This Little Piggy Went to the Beach

Have fun making new friends
♡
Nonnie Rose

Dedicated To: Ava, Nicholas, & Norah

Be kind, Have fun, Laugh a lot, and Watch the magic happen.

Acknowledgements

To my wonderful friends,

who are always looking for an adventure to unfold.

Based on a True Story

One sunny day, two friends, Sherry and Nonnie went for a walk to the beach. Along the way, they came across their friend, Max, who was walking with his dog. Walking right behind Max was a little pig. Sherry called out "Hi Max, did you get a new pet? A pig? Can we please pet your new piggy?"

Max said, "Sure you can pet her, but she isn't my piggy. She followed us here. I think she is lost!" The ladies looked at each other and said "OH NO! A lost piggy! We better find her family before she roams further away from home!" Max said he would take care of the little piggy while Sherry and Nonnie went to look for the pig's family.

Sherry and Nonnie went back to the street where they first saw the little piggy. The houses were all unique and very different, they were pink, and purple, and green, and all had different shapes. The ladies went to every house, and knocked on every door asking: "Are you missing a little piggy? There is a lost little pig at the beach!"

No one seemed to belong to the piggy; but everyone went to the beach to see the piggy.

After knocking on so many doors, Sherry and Nonnie came to a house with big purple tree, and a large vegetable garden. There were many different fruits and veggies, in different colors and sizes, all growing wild! The two friends looked at each other and with great joy said "This is a perfect garden for a piggy!" They rushed to the door and knocked as loudly as they could. KNOCK.....KNOCK....KNOCK...

A lady, who wore a bun on the top of her head, opened the door. She was quite surprised to hear about the piggy at the beach. "Yes, Yes !" she said, "that's my piggy! That's Harmonious, but I call her Harmony."

The lady said "I must find her right away! Would you please take me to her?" So off they went. The lady with the bun on her head used her cane to help her run faster.

So off to the beach they went to find Harmony.

Meanwhile, at the beach, everyone was enjoying the sun, and the warm sand, and the little piggy. This was the first time they met a pig at the beach. More and more people were gathering around the pig.

There were tall people, short people, little people, round people, and skinny people. Some people had pink skin, some brown skin, and some even had red skin! Some people walked, some used skateboards, others used bikes, wheelchairs and even surfboards to ride on the water! The piggy thought this was great !! "HOW EXCITING!" she thought. Harmony was amazed by all the different people !!

Harmony noticed a little girl in a pink swimsuit with a friendly smile and PIGTAILS too, pigtails by her ears! Now that was special! The little girl sat down and shared her lunch with Harmony. All the while, the little girl was admiring Harmony's pigtail.

Everyone was very curious about the piggy at the beach. Where did she come from?

All these different people reminded Harmony of the different plants, fruits, and veggies growing in her garden at home. There were tall trees, short trees, skinny shrubs and round shrubs. There were apples with green skins, yellow skins and even red skins. Some carrots were orange, others were purple. They were all different and special in their own way. She loved them all.

Running as fast as she could, Harmony's mom seemed to gain more and more speed by using her cane. The ladies couldn't keep up with her. She didn't stop for ice cream, she didn't even stop to talk to her friends, she just kept running. She could see a large crowd at the beach, and knew they were gathering around her little Harmony.

When she arrived at the beach, Harmony was very happy to see her mom. They ran to each other and hugged a big L-O-N-G hug. Max was still watching over Harmony while Harmony met some new friends. Harmony was sharing lunch with a new friend.

People kept asking: Is this your piggy? What's her name? The piggy's mom responded: This is little Harmonious, but I call her Harmony."

"Harmony! That's a beautiful name," said the little girl in the pink swimsuit. Harmony thought this little girl was special because she had never seen anyone with pigtails by their ears! Harmony knew they would be best friends forever.

Harmony and her mom spent the entire afternoon visiting with their new friends at the beach. As the sun started to set, they waved good bye to all their new friends, and promised to come back and visit with them at the beach. Harmony and her mom walked back home.

When they arrived home, Harmony laid down in her big garden. She fell asleep quickly and dreamed about playing with all her new friends, the pink ones, the brown ones, the short ones, and the tall ones, and her favorite one....the girl with the pigtails by her ears.

The End

CPSIA information can be obtained
at www.ICGtesting.com
Printed in the USA
BVHW061326150922
647089BV00001B/4